I0607824

EXPRESSIONS OF THE HEART

Inspirational Poems

LISA BRADLEY

Expressions of the Heart

Copyright

© Copyright 2016 by Lisa Bradley
All rights reserved.

This document is geared towards providing exact and reliable information in regards to the topic and issue covered. The publication is sold with the idea that the publisher is not required to render accounting, officially permitted, or otherwise, qualified services. If advice is necessary, legal or professional, a practiced individual in the profession should be ordered.

From a Declaration of Principles which was accepted and approved equally by a Committee of the American Bar Association and a Committee of Publishers and Associations.

In no way is it legal to reproduce, duplicate, or transmit any part of this document in either electronic means or in printed format. Recording of this publication is strictly

Expressions of the Heart

prohibited and any storage of this document is not allowed unless with written permission from the publisher. All rights reserved.

The information provided herein is stated to be truthful and consistent, in that any liability, in terms of inattention or otherwise, by any usage or abuse of any policies, processes, or directions contained within is the solitary and utter responsibility of the recipient reader. Under no circumstances will any legal responsibility or blame be held against the publisher for any reparation, damages, or monetary loss due to the information herein, either directly or indirectly.

Respective authors own all copyrights not held by the publisher.

The information herein is offered for informational purposes solely, and is universal as so. The presentation of the information is without contract or any type of guarantee assurance.

Expressions of the Heart

The trademarks that are used are without any consent, and the publication of the trademark is without permission or backing by the trademark owner. All trademarks and brands within this book are for clarifying purposes only and are the owned by the owners themselves, not affiliated with this document.

All Scripture quotation, unless otherwise indicated, are taken from the Holy Bible, New International Version□. NIV□. Copyright □ 1973, 1978, 1984 by International Bible Society. Used by permission of Zondervan Publishing House.

ISBN: 978-1-943409-15-0

All rights reserved.

Expressions of the Heart

Table of Contents

Expressions of the Heart

Expressions of the Heart

DEDICATION

This poetic journey was birthed from my life experiences and challenges. I dedicate this book to all who read it and pray it touches your life in some way.

Expressions of the Heart

ACKNOWLEDGEMENTS

I want to first honor my God for granting me this season to share with others what He placed in me. I am a firm believer that your gift will truly make room for you for He said "a gift opens the way and ushers the giver into the presence of the great" (Proverbs 18:16). Thank you Lord.

To my husband Mathis, my daughter Alisha, my mother Viola Shaw, my sister Kendra Shaw, my nieces Kaila Robertson and Kimberly Shaw, and my nephew Kobe Shaw. I thank all of you for your love and support. I could not have done this without you.

I also want to recognize my sister in Christ, Evangelist Traci Williamson. I appreciate your genuine friendship, words of encouragement and prayers. Thank you for always being there.

THE BIBLE

The Bible is a tool:

Just as a carpenter needs his hammer to repair and build a home,

A Christian needs the Bible to repair and build his life.

The Bible is a guide:

Just as a traveler needs his map, or a hiker needs his compass

to know what path, road, or turns to take, when to yield, and when to stop,

A Christian needs the Bible in their walk of life to know the same.

Expressions of the Heart

The Bible is a weapon:

Just as a policeman needs his gun to fight against criminals,

A Christian needs the Bible to fight against the enemy.

The Bible is medicine:

Just as a doctor prescribes a pill for a sick patient,

A Christian needs the Bible as prescription for sickness and healing.

The Bible is a defender:

Just as an offender needs a lawyer in a courtroom,

A Christian needs the Bible in times of trouble and persecution.

Expressions of the Heart

The Bible is protection:

Just as a homeless person needs a safe-haven,

A Christian needs the Bible for shelter and refuge in times of storm.

The Bible is a source and foundation for all things.

The Bible is the way to live and the way to be if you want to see Jesus Christ.

The Bible is all true and all-powerful.

The Bible is the light that can shine upon and open up the darkest soul.

The Bible is Sacred.

The Bible is Holy.

Expressions of the Heart

The Bible is the Word of God.

The Bible is God.

Expressions of the Heart

I AM NOT WORTHY

For the things I've done or didn't do

For the things I've said or didn't say

For the things I've thought or didn't think

I am not worthy!

For the times I didn't fast

For the times I didn't pray

For the times I didn't read my Bible

I am not worthy!

For the times I didn't praise

For the times I didn't sing

Expressions of the Heart

For the times I didn't encourage

I am not worthy!

For the times I didn't forgive

For the times I didn't forget

For the times I didn't let go

I am not worthy!

For the times I didn't give

For the times I didn't help

For the times I didn't visit

I am not worthy!

For the times I didn't listen

For the times I didn't learn

For the times I didn't ask for forgiveness

Expressions of the Heart

I am not worthy!

For the times I didn't like

For the times I didn't love

For the times I didn't care

I am not worthy!

For the times I didn't move

For the times I didn't wait

For the times I didn't let God

I am not worthy!

For God gave His only Son

For Jesus was crucified for my sins

For He died so that I may live

He is worthy!

Expressions of the Heart

MOTHER

I thank God for blessing me with a mother like you.

You are a perfect example of what living for Christ will do.

You showed me that there is more to life than money or material things.

It's all about the love of Jesus, and all the joy that He brings.

Your unselfish ways and generous heart have helped so many.

Expressions of the Heart

If they were without a dime, you would give them your last penny.

There have been many hard times and even a little pain. God never said that there would never be any rain.

You have been tried and tested, and tested and tried. There was nothing you could not handle with God on your side.

So many have wondered how you got where you are today. You knew in your heart that it was Jesus who paved the way.

Expressions of the Heart

All glory, honor, and praise belong to Him, and Him alone.

Without His grace and mercy, you could not have made it on your own.

God has appointed and anointed you as His chosen one.

He has blessed you over and over for loving His only Son.

Continue to praise God, from where all your blessings flow.

For the one and only God you serve has the very last say so.

So when people start to question why and how you made it this far,

Expressions of the Heart

Let them know that it was God's favor that got you where you are.

THANK YOU MY FRIEND

When I didn't know

When I didn't see

Thank you.

When I didn't want to

When I didn't think

Thank you.

When I felt uncomfortable

When I felt unsure

Thank you.

Expressions of the Heart

When I didn't trust

When I didn't care

Thank you.

When I felt frustrated

When I felt burdened

Thank you.

Thank you, my friend, for being trustworthy.

Thank you, my friend, for being honest.

Thank you, my friend, for always having my back.

Thank you, my friend, for being a support system.

Thank you, my friend, for having faith in me.

Thank you, my friend, for encouraging me.

Expressions of the Heart

Thank you, my friend, for listening to me.

Thank you, my friend, for just being you.

Expressions of the Heart

I'LL MISS YOU

My journey here has come to an end, and now it's time to go.

But before I leave this place, there are some things I want you to know.

I have enjoyed my time here, and the friendships I've made.

I know that some will continue on and never fade.

God sent me here for a time and a season.

For He alone knows the purpose and the reason.

I have shared many talks, laughs, and even cries.

Expressions of the Heart

But I knew at some point, I would have to say my good-byes.

I have grown personally and professionally, and learned a lot while here.

For all of you, I will remember, cherish, and hold close and dear.

I have stretched myself to do things I never thought I could do.

For God always had my back, and without hesitation He saw me through.

Every one of you has tugged at my heart in one way or another.

For this experience has truly, without a doubt, been like no other.

Expressions of the Heart

So I thank all of you, and wish you nothing but success.

And remember, I love you, but my God loves you best.

SISTER

We've known each other for so many years.

We've shared some laughs and even some tears.

You've had some tests, and even failed a few.

But that's something we all have to go through.

As long as you keep God as the head,

He will always do what He said.

So don't worry about people and what they say.

You know that God will always, not sometimes, make a

way.

Expressions of the Heart

Life brings many challenges, to test our faith and commitment to Him.

This is to keep us focused, don't make decisions on a whim.

We all have trials and tribulations that make us grow strong.

With God as the person in charge of your life, you can never go wrong.

I know that sometimes you may feel like you're all alone.

But remember that you have God first, then family and friends to call your own.

You are beautiful, inside and out, and very intelligent too.

Expressions of the Heart

I only want the best and all that God has for you.

God has something very special for you to do.

He will, at the appointed time, make it known to you.

Your visions and dreams are only the beginning.

Give God the glory first, and He will make sure you come out winning.

So remember that God says that you can have what you say.

Therefore, I say you are abundantly loved and blessed in every way.

MARRIAGE

Marriage is the ultimate tie that binds.

It connects a man and woman's heart, body, soul, and mind.

Marriage is loving in spite of, and not because of - unconditionally.

Loving through the good, the bad, and even the ugly.

Marriage is apologizing even when you know you've done nothing wrong.

Having compassion and respect will only make your bond strong.

Expressions of the Heart

Marriage is being honest, even if it brings a little pain.

Even the best of couples at some point share a little rain.

Marriage is communicating, even when you don't want to talk.

Listening, not just hearing, will help your matrimonial walk.

Marriage is a commitment and dedication for life.

Devotion and honor between a husband and his wife.

Marriage is a gift from God that requires much prayer.

It's understanding, forgiving, open-mindedness, and care.

Expressions of the Heart

Marriage is compromising, and not just doing things your way.

You have to be considerate and conscientious of what you say.

Marriage is not about what's yours is yours, and what's mine is mine.

It's about sharing, giving, sacrificing, and being kind.

Marriage is not being separate, and it's all about being together and having fun.

You are no longer considered two individuals, but as a powerful one.

So just remember to keep God first in everything you do

Expressions of the Heart

And He will keep your marriage and continuously bless you.

THANK YOU AUNT BELL

Aunt Bell, as she is often called

She always answers with a smile

She will do whatever is asked of her

She goes that extra mile

She helps the family out a lot

Whenever you need her, she's always there

From taking mom to doctor visits

To babysitting, or even braiding hair

She gives so much of herself

She's a blessing from God above

Expressions of the Heart

She truly believes in family

And doing things for the ones you love

She asks for nothing in return

She does things from the heart

I could never truly repay

But saying "thank you" is a start

Thank you also goes to Uncle Ralph

For being unselfish and kind

Not many husbands would understand

A wife giving so much of her time

It's better to give than to receive, Aunt Bell

You reap what you sow

As you are rewarded for what you've given

Expressions of the Heart

Your blessings will be in the overflow

MY SISTER, MY FRIEND

My Sister, My Friend

Wipe all of those tears away

God is all you need to get you through the day

My Sister, My Friend

Hold your head up high and smile

It will all be over after while

My Sister, My Friend

I know you are weary and tired

But keep in mind that much is given, much is required

Expressions of the Heart

My Sister, My Friend

You are going through for a reason

It's about to be your time and season

My Sister, My Friend

Satan knows that you are about to be blessed

That's why he doesn't want you to pass this test

My Sister, My Friend

Let God handle it from the start

He will give you peace to guard your mind and heart

My Sister, My Friend

Let go and let God, don't try to fix it yourself

God is Lord and He doesn't need our help

Expressions of the Heart

My Sister, My Friend

Put your trust and faith in no man

God is the only one who truly can

So My Sister, My Friend

When you're feeling low and don't know who to turn to

Remember that God is the only one that can and will see

you through

Expressions of the Heart

BLESS THIS HOUSE

Bless this house, from the ceiling to the floor.

Bless this house, from every room to every door.

Bless this house, and all that reside,

Bless this house, and may God continue to be by your side.

Bless this house, from every angle and every direction.

Bless this house, and cover it, Lord, with your protection.

Bless this house, from the foundation to the roof.

Bless this house with goodness and truth.

Expressions of the Heart

Bless this house with your peace and your love.

Bless this house with your grace from above.

Bless this house, and keep this family from danger and harm.

Bless this house, and may they always be safe from the storm.

Bless this house when times are good and when times are bad.

Bless this house, and know that He has made you glad.

Bless this house and everything that is in it.

Bless this house in the name of the Father, the Son, and the Holy Spirit.

WELL WISHES

I wish you well and much success

For your life has just begun.

Thank you so much for everything

You've been a blessing to everyone.

Your time with us was not long

But we've grown to love you so.

Your sweet and humble spirit was noticed

As soon as you walked through our door.

Your beautiful smile and warm heart

Was so evident and clear.

Expressions of the Heart

For it was not luck or chance,

But God who sent you here.

Everything is predestined in this world

Nothing "just happens", but is planned.

You were placed in our paths for a reason

To touch someone's life, or just to lend a helping hand.

As you move forward in your career

And in your relationship with our Savior.

Do not forget that He is the I AM

And can bless you with much favor.

Life will get hard sometimes,

And the enemy will try to keep you bound.

Expressions of the Heart

Be encouraged and remember you know an awesome Man

That will never let you down.

I pray for nothing but goodness for you and your family

As you leave today from this place,

May God forever keep you in His care

And cover you with His mercy and grace.

WILSON FAMILY PRAYER

We purposed in our hearts

To come together and pray

We knew without hesitation

That prayer was the only way

To loosen the tight grip

Of Satan's heavy hand

We had to call on the name of Jesus

To mess up the devil's plan

To destroy and kill

What he thought was his

Expressions of the Heart

But he had to be reminded

That God still is

Most Faithful, All Powerful

Merciful and True

For with the Almighty

We knew we would make it through

Yes, all families have trials

And go through many things

But it's all in how you handle them

That determines what life brings

We chose to give it to God

And let Him have His way

We knew once He took control

Expressions of the Heart

Everything would be okay

We've been praying long and hard

Strong, never doubting or ceasing

We knew that God would do what He said

As long as we continued to do what was pleasing

We've been blessed so much as a family

And we thank Him for everything

But we are believing in God

To do more awesome and miraculous things

Our family has grown stronger

And closer to the Lord

Because we came together agreeing

And praying on one accord

Expressions of the Heart

It's been some time since we began

And we are still going strong

A family that prays together stays together

The Wilson Family has proven that not to be wrong

WELCOME HOME

You've been gone for a while

But we knew it wouldn't be long

Before God would safely

Bring you back home

The family never ceased praying

We did what we had to do

For we knew our prayers would avail

And God would see us through

All of this happened for a reason

It was a part of God's master plan

Expressions of the Heart

To get you in a position

That would humble you and make you understand

God has an assignment for you to complete

Whether or not you believe it to be true

And at the appointed time

He will show you what you need to do

So you need to recognize

That you are truly blessed

Just turn everything over to God

And He will handle the rest

Welcome Home!

BECAUSE HE LOVES ME

He was born and crucified

He died for my sins

He will return again

Because He loves me

I shall live and not die

I am forgiven and set free

I am loved unconditionally

Because He loves me

I have joy in my soul

I have love in my heart

Expressions of the Heart

I have been humbled

Because He loves me

I have grace and mercy

I have power and authority

I am healed

Because He loves me

I am abundantly blessed

I pray and not worry

I have a peace that surpasses all understanding

Because He loves me

I believe all things are possible

I can see beyond the natural

I have faith the size of a mustard seed

Expressions of the Heart

Because He loves me

I can speak those things that are not, as though they were

I have favor in everything

I have eternal life

Because He loves me

Because He loves me

I can do all things through Christ that strengthens me

TRUTH IS

Truth Is

I haven't always done right

But I know God still loves me

Truth Is

I haven't always made good decisions

But I know God still cares for me

Truth Is

I haven't always been good

But I know God forgives me

Expressions of the Heart

Truth Is

I am not the perfect Christian

But I know God is preparing me

Truth Is

I know I am not where I need to be

But I know God is working on getting me there

And the truth has been spoken!

GOD IS

God is

      a comforter

      a provider

      a healer

      a defender

God is

      shelter

      protection

      family

      friend

Expressions of the Heart

God is

      truth

      honesty

      integrity

      righteous

God is

      all-knowing

      all-seeing

      all-powerful

      all-true

God is

      happiness

      peace

      kindness

Expressions of the Heart

forgiveness

God is

understanding

caring

compassion

love

God simply is

LOVE IS

Love is
  Real
    Free
      Risky
        Hurtful
          Deserving
            Faithful
              Togetherness
              Good
                Beautiful
                Awesome
                True
                  Compromising
                  Respectful
                    Passionate
                    Mature (Sometimes)
                    Communication
                    Bold
                    Undeniable
                    Connected

Expressions of the Heart

Considerate

Weary

Giving

LOVE IS GOD!

Expressions of the Heart

A SPIRIT BROKEN

My spirit has been broken

My heart has been crushed

My dreams and desires, I want no more

I just want to give up

My spirit has been broken

My heart torn up inside

My mind is restless and heavy

I just want to run and hide

My spirit has been broken

My prayers seem to go unheard

My life feels barren and dry

Expressions of the Heart

Sometimes it's hard to hear His word

My spirit has been broken

My joy inside has faded

I feel as though I'm going through the motions

Like my life is just a big charade

My spirit has been broken

But I must find my way back

To the only one who can help me

Get back on the right track

My spirit has been broken

But this sadness has to go away

So I can praise Him as I ought to

And diligently seek Him everyday

Expressions of the Heart

My spirit has been broken

But I feel that God sees my tears

I know He hears me when I cry

I just need to pray away my fears

My spirit has been broken

But my faith has to let me see

Beyond the right-now situation

For I know God is there for me

My spirit has been broken

But now it's time to mend

These pieces of a shattered soul

So in me a new life can begin

Expressions of the Heart

My spirit has been broken

But no longer a broken spirit am I

The spirit of brokenness is over

Broken spirit, I say to you, goodbye

CALL ON HIM

When you feel all alone

And think you have no one to talk to

Call on Him

When the one friend you thought you had

Turns their back on you

Call on Him

When you lose your job

After working there all your life

Call on Him

Expressions of the Heart

When your money is low

And all of your bills are due

Call on Him

When you get sick

And the doctor has given up on you

Call on Him

Call on Him when you need a comforter

Call on Him when you need a true friend

Call on Him when you need shelter

Call on Him when you need a provider

Call on Him when you need a healer

Just call on Him!

MY CHILD

Lord, I give my daughter back to You

I cannot bear this heavy burden alone

I need Your guidance and direction

To bring my daughter safely home

Physically, mentally, emotionally, spiritually

I need her to come back completely whole

But only You can perform this miracle

And bring her back, pure as gold

Growing up, but not all grown up

With attitude in tow

Expressions of the Heart

Not realizing that one day some of our actions

Would alter the life we know

I pray, Lord God, that You will protect her

As she travels this unfamiliar territory

Knowing that when the time is right

Her testimony will be her story

Of how she overcame the struggles and pressures

In this mean and evil world

And how God intervened and took control

Of the life of this teenage girl

Congratulations

My sister, it's been a long time coming

But you did what you set out to do

To fulfill the vision and the dream

God specifically gave to you

I know at times it seemed as if

It would never come to pass

But when God sets you up for something

He will always make sure you finish the task

Your gifts and talents are making room

For you to do God's will

Expressions of the Heart

All you had to do was wait

Patiently and stand still

Yes, there will be those who just won't get it

And find it hard to understand

How and why it happened this way

Just tell them it was all a part of God's plan

To follow the path He set for you

To encourage, uplift, and speak a word

To share with all who would listen

Throughout this land, your voice will be heard

Your anointing will impact the lives of many

You took heed and answered the call

People will be inspired and know without a doubt

Expressions of the Heart

That in God's house, they can have it all

He has much more in store for you

You won't be able to contain

The abundant overflow He has for your life

And humble, I know you will remain

I am very proud of what you've done

And I see only great things ahead

You are a true testament to everyone

That God will do just what He said

I am glad that I came to know you

You've become a part of my family

God allowed me a chance to call you "friend"

And I thank Him so much for the opportunity

Expressions of the Heart

So I pray for you and your blessings

Great success, and so much love

You can truly have what you say

If you keep your mind on Him above

Expressions of the Heart

BATTLE WITHIN

I feel like I am caught in the middle

And my back is against the wall

I'm being pulled in all directions

And it's all I can do not to fall

Face first in the dirt

Struggling with the emotions within

A battle I often wonder

If I'm ever going to win

I know the war is only within me

Fighting the enemy inside

Things I thought would just go away

Expressions of the Heart

But in me they still reside

In my heart and in my mind

Not going, but wanting to stay

Lingering dangerously from the past

In my soul, just eating away

I feel overwhelmed

Uncertain and unsure

If I'm strong enough to handle

If I will be able to endure

Bad things do happen to good people

Or am I just reaping what I sow

Did I bring all of this on myself

From past choices, sometimes I think so

Expressions of the Heart

My mind is constantly going

Trying to understand

Why I feel the way I do

When I profess to be a Christian

Then I had to realize

That Christians are humans too

Sometimes we allow the flesh to overtake us

Instead of just praying our way through

Although sometimes I may feel a little defeated

And the devil may think he's won

But he has to know that for the God I serve

The battle has just begun

Expressions of the Heart

I am just waiting on the manifestation

Because I know it's already done

I've got the victory in Jesus Christ

The one and only begotten Son

THINGS ARE ABOUT TO CHANGE

Things are about to change

Your struggle will be over soon

Satan thought he had you

But God is stepping in to prove that

Things are about to change

Your blessings are on the way

Just speak those things into existence

Because you can have what you say

Things are about to change

Expressions of the Heart

What you thought you couldn't do, you can

God is making a way out of no way

Remember, He has the master plan

Things are about to change

The enemy has no power

In what your life will become

God is your strong tower

Things are about to change

Your dreams will come to pass

God said anything you want

In His name, all you have to do is ask

Things are about to change

No matter what lies ahead

Expressions of the Heart

God will make everything alright

Just have faith, and believe He'll do what He said

Things are about to change

Your finances will be blessed

Prosperity and healing are on the way

God only wants to give you the best

Things are about to change

There is no limit to what God can do

All things are possible with Him as your guide

He will always see you through

Things are about to change

A new day has begun

Soon the darkness will pass away

Expressions of the Heart

Because the victory has already been won

Yes, things are about to change!

WARNING BEFORE DESTRUCTION

We often say we didn't see it coming

We saw no warning or sign

But if we take a moment to think back, we actually saw

the signals the entire time

I guess I didn't want to admit

Or just didn't want to believe

That things were starting to take a turn, in a direction I

did not want to receive

But only if I'd begun to pray

At the very first sign of attack

Expressions of the Heart

Then maybe the enemy wouldn't have slipped in like he did, sneaking behind my back

Trying to steal what was mine

My family, my life

Challenging me beyond measures, as a mother and a wife

God always warns us

Of things yet to come

I just didn't take heed to the alarm, or thought Satan wouldn't try to put me on the run

That feeling, that urge

That dream, that vision

That awareness that something just wasn't right was only the beginning

Expressions of the Heart

God tapped me on the shoulder

With the first hit, I shrugged it off

The second tap was a little harder, but I still didn't

answer the call

But by the third time

It was too late

No more soft tapping, but a hard hitting punch in the face

He tried to remind me

That I needed to pray

To read His word without fail, and talk to Him everyday

All those times He was trying to get

My attention and make me see

Expressions of the Heart

I was getting comfortable in my doings, and not making

Him my priority

My disobedience led to destruction

Circumstances beyond my control

All I had to do was heed the warning and begin to pray

like I'd never prayed before

But I now take notice of the little things

And begin to pray and rebuke the enemy

So little things might not blow up into big things, and

cause harm and devastation to my family

GOD GIVES PERMISSION

God gives the enemy permission

To make us take a stand

He allows him to attack us

And try us on every hand

God gives the enemy permission

To bring us some heartache and pain

To test our mustard seed of faith

By sending us some heavy rain

God gives the enemy permission

To attempt to steal and destroy

Expressions of the Heart

Our lives, family, friends

Happiness and joy

God gives the enemy permission

To knock us down to see

If we have what it takes to get back up

And without fear, face the adversary

God gives the enemy permission

To take us to our knees

To get us praying with much avail

And relying on Him totally

God gives the enemy permission

So He can take us to another level

To get us to where He would have us be

Expressions of the Heart

And to use our authority to flee the devil

God gives the enemy permission

To push us beyond measure

And make us give Him back His word

And bring out those hidden treasures

God gives the enemy permission

To take us out of our comfort zone

To get us to do things in our lives

 We haven't done before

God gives the enemy permission

To get us to be ruthless and bold

To speak His word and not waver

And let the devil know who is in control

Expressions of the Heart

God gives the enemy permission

So our lives can be transformed

Renewed, restored, and redeemed

To glorify His name with praise, forever more

Weary Soul

A weary soul knows no rest

It's uneasy and unsure

It's restless and has no peace

Not much more can it endure

A weary soul knows no rest

It's weakened from its trials

It has little faith, or none at all

Unable to hold its fire

A weary soul knows no rest

Tiresome and sleepless nights

Expressions of the Heart

Worn, wavered, and straddled

Unable to put up a fight

A weary soul knows no rest

Not able to stand the storm

Lonely, heartbroken, and divided

Feeling hopeless and all alone

A weary soul knows no rest

Confused, and questions why

Unable to understand this trying season

As the years slowly drift by

A weary soul knows no rest

Unsettled with fear

Crazy ideas and thoughts try to overtake

Expressions of the Heart

As loneliness draws near

A weary soul knows no rest

In a state of frustration and tears

Unable to shake this way of being

Fighting hard to pray away the fears

A weary soul knows no rest

But if I rest in You

My soul is revived again

Refreshed and brand new

Forgive Me

Forgive me, Father, for I have sinned

My life should be a reflection of You

But sometimes with my thoughts and the things I say

That does not always hold true

Forgive me, Father, for I have sinned

I am supposed to let my light shine

But my worries and cares are sometimes put first

As I should cast all upon Thine

Forgive me, Father, for I have sinned

My life, I want in Your will

Expressions of the Heart

But my words and actions don't always show

How my life to You I give

Forgive me, Father, for I have sinned

My prayers and praise sometimes cease

My faith wavers, shakes, and often falters

When my life should be filled with peace

Forgive me, Father, for I have sinned

My thoughts and ways are not always good

But I must plead the blood and rebuke the enemy

And praise You like I should

Forgive me, Father, for I have sinned

Going to church has become a chore

No feeling, no praying, no Bible

Expressions of the Heart

But I desire and long for so much more

Forgive me, Father, for I have sinned

Allowing my distractions to be put before You

When I know that You should be priority

To help guide me and bring me through

Forgive me, Father, for I have sinned

But I know, because of You

I am forgiven for all of my wrongs

For Your Grace and Mercy are true

Expressions of the Heart

Why Not Me

Everyone has heartache and pain

I should be no different

Why not me

Everyone has that thorn or wound

That is hard to hide or heal

Why not me

Everyone has their cross to bear

Their season of tribulation

Why not me

Expressions of the Heart

Everyone has lost a friend or loved one

Bringing about confusion and anguish

Why not me

Everyone has had a broken heart or two

Shattered almost beyond repair

Why not me

Everyone has to go through something

Some very tough and trying times

Why not me

Life is all about seasons

Everyone has to go through them

Why not me

Expressions of the Heart

Why not me Lord

Why not me

Expressions of the Heart

What Was and Now Is

I think about what was

Young, innocent, happy

I think about what is now

Older, settled, content

I think about what was

Laughter, love, joy

I think about what is now

Muffled, angry, misunderstood

I think about what was

Peace, communication, respectful

I think about what is now

Expressions of the Heart

Confusion, quiet, hurt

I think about what was

Affection, sharing, considerate

I think about what is now

Disconnect, separate, selfish

I think about what was

Prayer, praise, worship

I think about was is now

Darkness, worry, uneasy

What was is no longer

And what now is has taken over

I want to get back to what was

And get rid of what is now

FAITH versus FEAR

Fear is FAITHLESS

Faith is FEARLESS

Fear CANCELS Faith

Faith REMOVES Fear

Fear promotes WORRY

Faith increases PRAYER

Fear BOUNDS you to the struggles of this life

Faith RELEASES you to live through the battles that exist

Expressions of the Heart

Fear SUFFOCATES, PARALYZES, IMMOBILIZES, and SEALS the mind

Faith FREES, RENEWS, TRANSFORMS, and OPENS the soul

Fear fosters LACK, DOUBT, and DEFEAT

Faith nurtures ABUNDANCE, CERTAINTY, and TRIUMPH

Transporting the BURDEN of Fear is HEAVY and OVERWHELMING

Carrying the WEIGHT of Faith is EFFORTLESS and POWERFUL

Both cost nothing to OBTAIN

But only one costs everything to MAINTAIN

Expressions of the Heart

So the question REMAINS

How will you LIVE

By FAITH or in FEAR

Expressions of the Heart

About the Author

Lisa Bradley is from Bishopville, South Carolina. She is married to Mathis Bradley and together they have one daughter, Alisha Nycole Bradley. Lisa is a graduate of Central Carolina Technical College and Morris College, and is currently pursuing a Masters degree in Education Technology from Webster University. While attending Morris, she was asked by one of her professors to put into words what she thought the Bible meant to her and she did so in the form of a poem. Little did she know that this Biblical Perspectives class would be the beginning of her writing journey. God used that class back in 2001 to start the process of what He knew was to come that would help her get through life's trials. He opened up something in her she never knew she had. Lisa began writing inspirational poems for special events and occasions, and family but then things started to happen

Expressions of the Heart

that led her to use poetry as an expression of what she was going through and feeling at certain times in her life. It allowed her to have a level of freedom. Like singing it became therapeutic. She started writing later in life than most however, God's timing is perfect. He knew what she needed even when she didn't. He knew this would be her way of escape, her peace and she thanks Him for it all. To God Be the Glory!

Pure Thoughts Publishing, LLC

Pure Thoughts Publishing, LLC

www.purethoughtspublishingllc.com

www.ingramcontent.com/pod-product-compliance
Lightning Source LLC
Chambersburg PA
CBHW051924220626
47052CB00003B/563